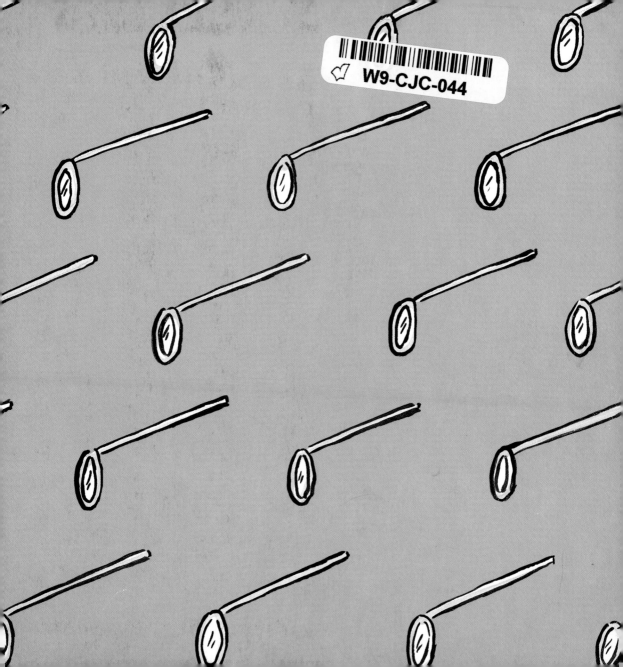

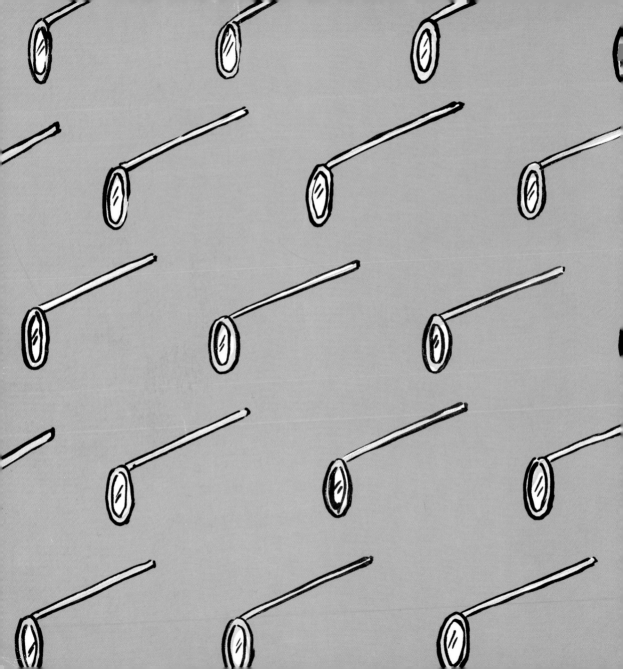

DOES A TIGER OPEN WIDE?

Fred Ehrlich, M.D.
Pictures by Emily Bolam

🍎 Blue Apple Books

Brooklyn, NY

With thanks to Dr. Spiegel,
for her careful review of the
text and pictures.

Text copyright © 2003 by Fred Ehrlich, M.D.
Illustrations copyright © 2003 by Emily Bolam
All rights reserved
CIP Data is available

Blue Apple Books
An affiliate of Handprint Books
413 Sixth Avenue, Brooklyn, New York 11215
www.handprintbooks.com

First Edition
Printed in China
ISBN: 1-929766-78-5

1   3   5   7   9   10   8   6   4   2

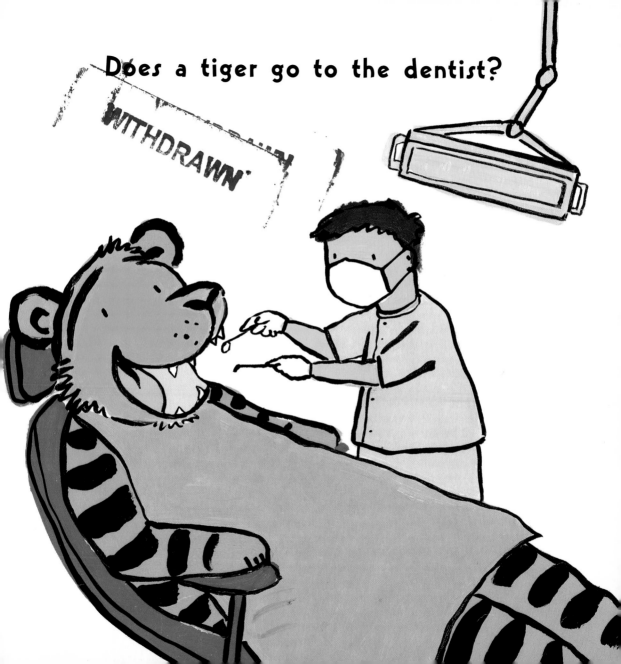

Oh, no!
A tiger won't sit in a dentist's chair.

No way!
A giraffe won't wear a dentist's bib,
or cooperate for a checkup.

Does a baboon go to the dentist?

Surely not!
A baboon would not allow the dentist
to put instruments in his mouth.

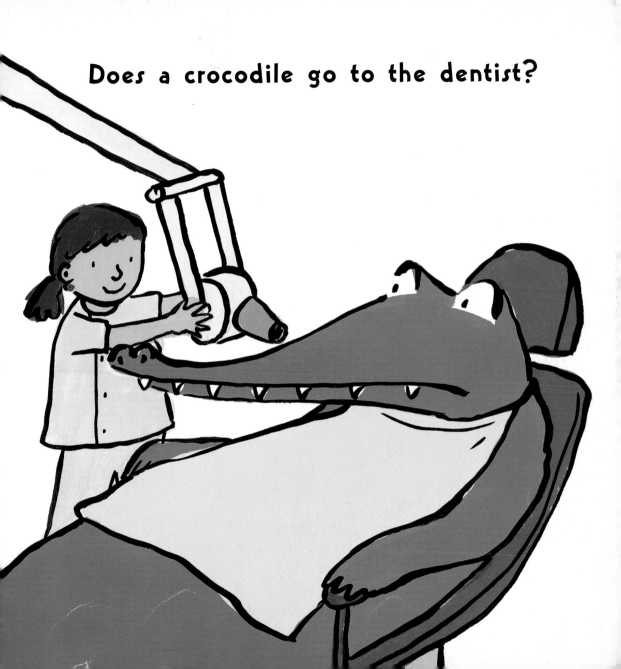

Does a crocodile go to the dentist?

Never!
A crocodile would never permit
the dentist to take pictures of his teeth.

Does a wolf go to the dentist
to get his teeth cleaned?

No, no!
A wolf would not allow a cleaning
of his teeth. A wolf's teeth get cleaned
by chewing and gnawing.

Do puppies get fluoride treatments
to keep their teeth strong and healthy?

No. Puppies don't get
their teeth painted with
fluoride to prevent cavities.

Animals don't usually get cavities.
But people do.

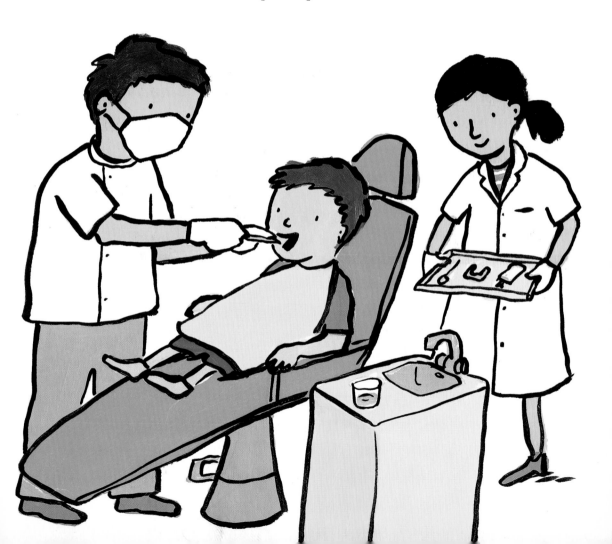

A person needs to go to the dentist
for a checkup at least once a year.

NO

And if the dentist finds a cavity,
the hole needs to be drilled and filled.

Mommies go to the dentist.
Daddies go.

Big kids go.
Little kids go.

Emily is not afraid of the dentist.
She knows what's going to happen
at the dentist's office.

And she knows she'll get a surprise when she's done.

Dr. Dan says people should take care
of their teeth with regular checkups.

Steps in a checkup:

dentist examines
teeth with explorer
and mirror

dentist x-rays teeth

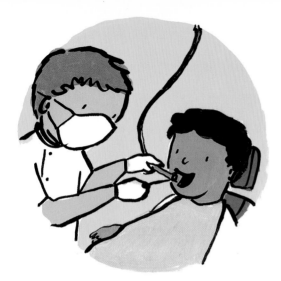

dentist cleans and
polishes teeth

dentist gives
toothbrush
and explains
how to take
care of your
teeth

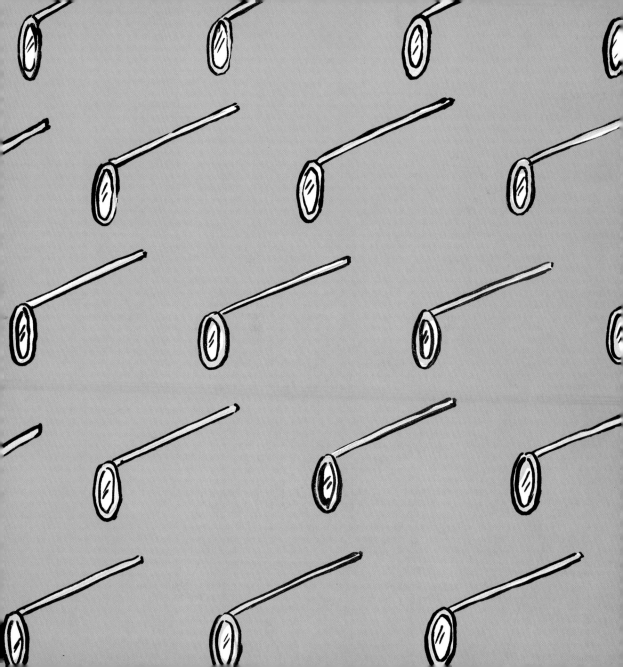

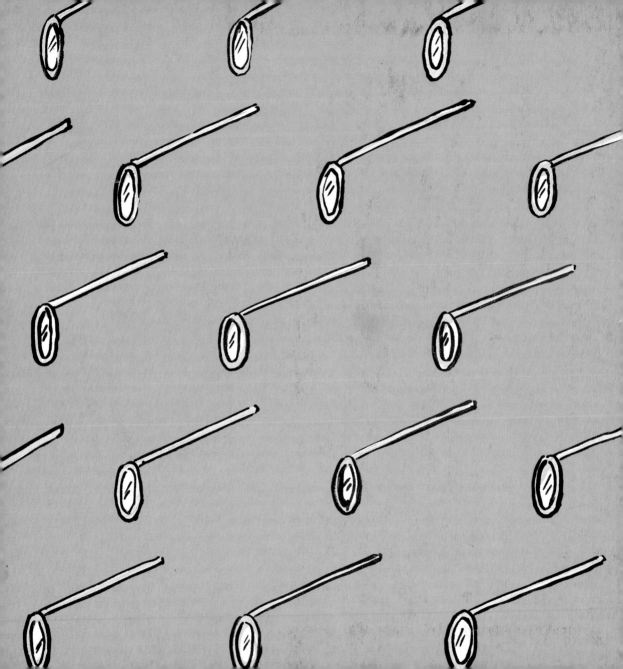